HELLO K

A Day with Papa

ABRADALE

New York

Hello Kitty loved weekends!
She gave Papa a hug.

Papa looked up from his book. He suggested that they spend the day together, but what should they do?

Hello Kitty thought of all the things that she liked best. Should they plant flowers in the garden? No, they did that last week. Should they see a movie? No, it was much too nice a day to spend indoors. Hello Kitty decided that they should play outside!

Hello Kitty asked Papa to teach her how to play baseball, so they could play together.

Hello Kitty wrote a note for Mama and her sister, Mimmy.

Papa and Hello Kitty walked to the sports shop.

**Papa found the baseball gloves and balls.
There were so many to choose from!**

When they got to the park, Papa showed
Hello Kitty how to hold the bat. He tossed
the ball to her. Hello Kitty swung and hit
the ball!

Next, they played catch. Papa threw the ball to Hello Kitty, and she caught it!

Hello Kitty and Papa played catch until it was time for lunch. Then they each had a hot dog and a cold drink.

Just as Hello Kitty finished her hot dog, she saw her friends Joey, Fifi, Tracy, and Jodie. What a wonderful surprise! When Hello Kitty's friends saw that she was playing baseball with Papa, they all got very excited and decided to play together.

They took their places on the field. When Joey pitched the ball to Hello Kitty, she hit it out of the park! Hello Kitty hit a home run! Hooray!

When Hello Kitty and her friends finished playing, Papa and Hello Kitty walked home. Papa told Hello Kitty how proud he was of her and what a good job she had done. Hello Kitty was so happy that Papa was proud of her. Hello Kitty enjoyed playing baseball with Papa! What a wonderful way to spend the day.

ISBN 978-1-4197-0649-3

Printed and bound in China
10 9 8 7 6 5 4 3 2

THE ART OF BOOKS SINCE 1949
115 West 18th Street
New York, NY 10011
www.abramsbooks.com